Andersen Press · London
Hutchinson Australia

NO ROOM TO SWING A CAT

To the one and only Nicholas

British Library Cataloguing in Publication Data
Steadman, Ralph
No room to swing a cat
I. Title
823'.914 [J]
ISBN 0-86264-241-8

© 1989 by Ralph Steadman
First published in Great Britain in 1989
by Andersen Press Ltd., 62-65 Chandos Place, London WC2.
Published in Australia by Century Hutchinson Australia Pty. Ltd.,
89-91 Albion Street, Surry Hills, NSW 2010.
All rights reserved. Colour separated in Switzerland
by Photolitho AG Offsetreproduktionen, Gossau, Zürich.
Printed in Italy by Grafiche AZ, Verona.

"My room's too small," said Tom.

"What d'you
mean, love?"
asked his
mother.

"My room's too small.

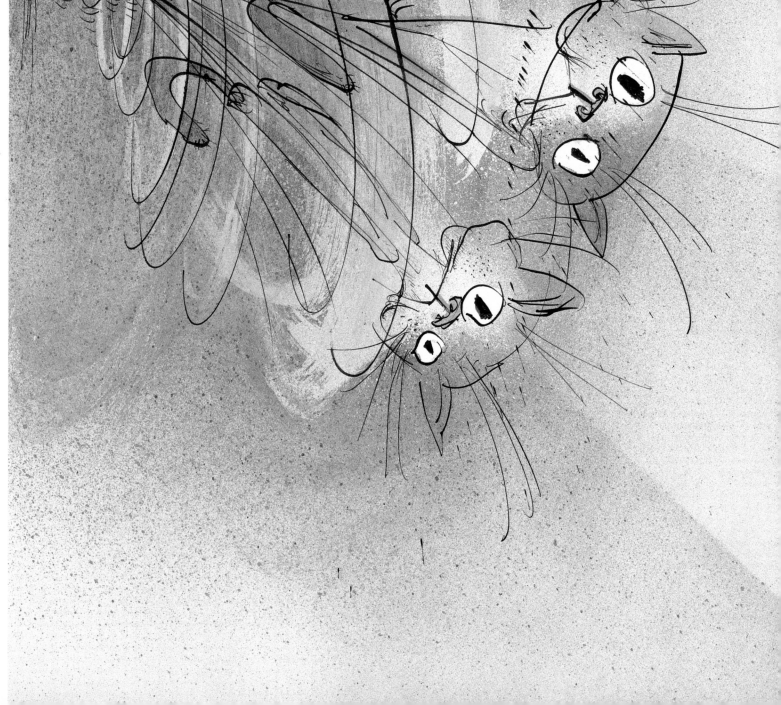

"There's not even room to swing a cat."

"What d'you want to swing a cat for?" said his mother.
"I don't," said Tom, "but my room's too small."

"Well, how big do you want it?" asked his mother.
"Very big," said Tom.

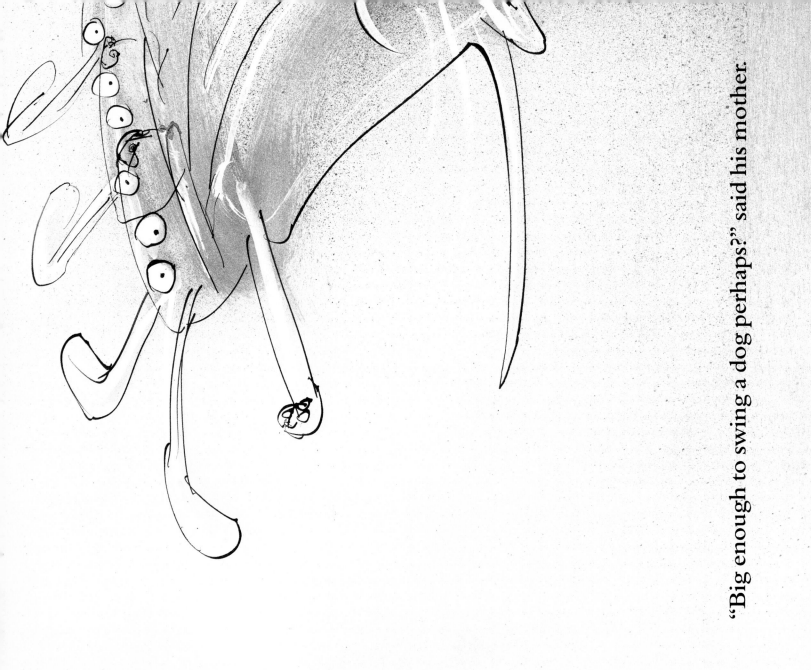

"Big enough to swing a dog perhaps?" said his mother.

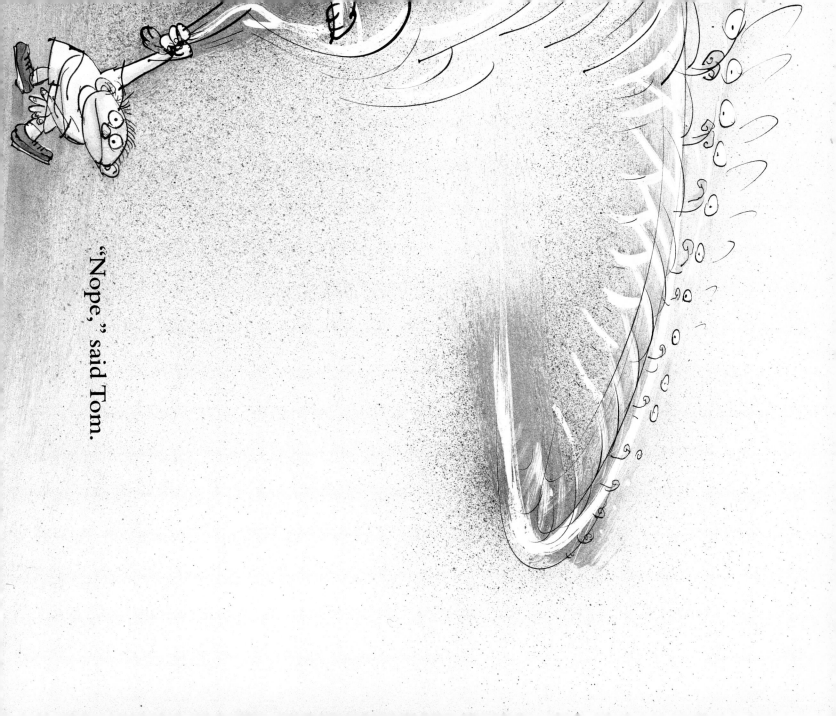

"Nope," said Tom.

"Big enough to swing a pig?" said his mother.

"Nope," said Tom.

"Big enough to swing a donkey, then?" said his mother.
"Nope," said Tom.

"Big enough to swing me?" she giggled. So did Tom.

"How about a horse?" said his mother.

"Nope," said Tom.

"A moose?" said
his mother.
"Nope," said Tom.

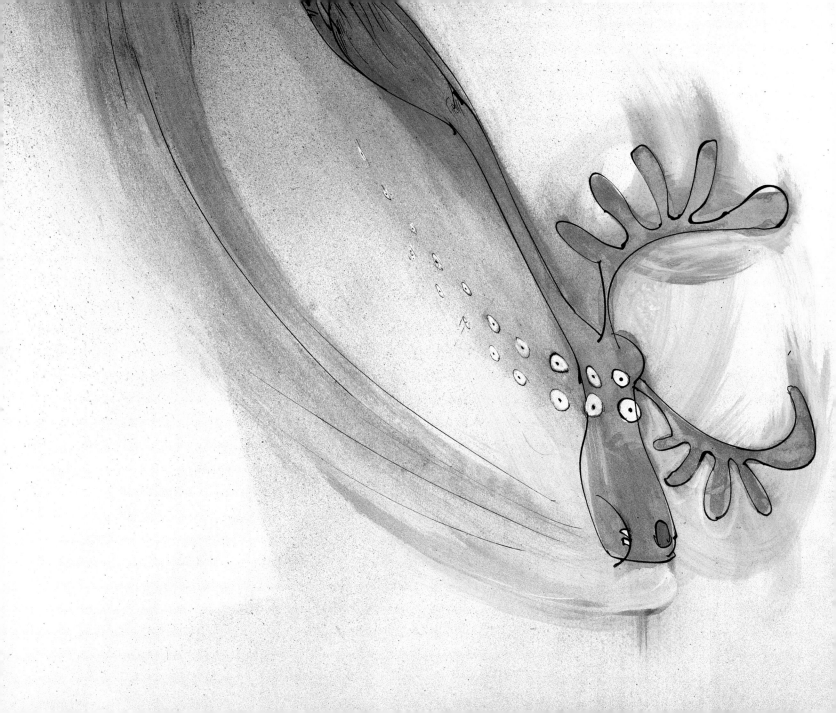

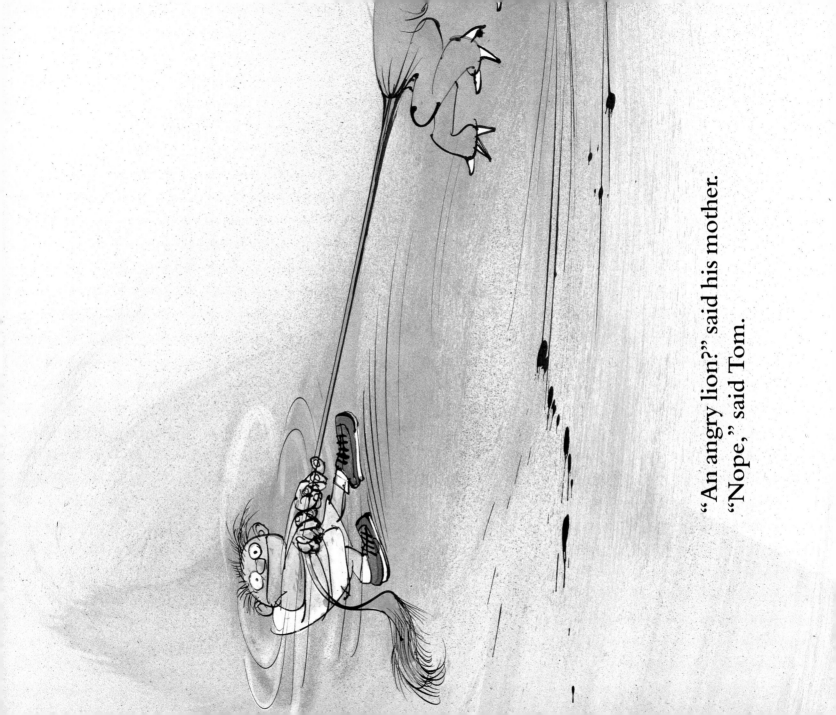

"An angry lion?" said his mother.
"Nope," said Tom.

"All right, an elephant?" said his mother.
"Nope," said Tom.

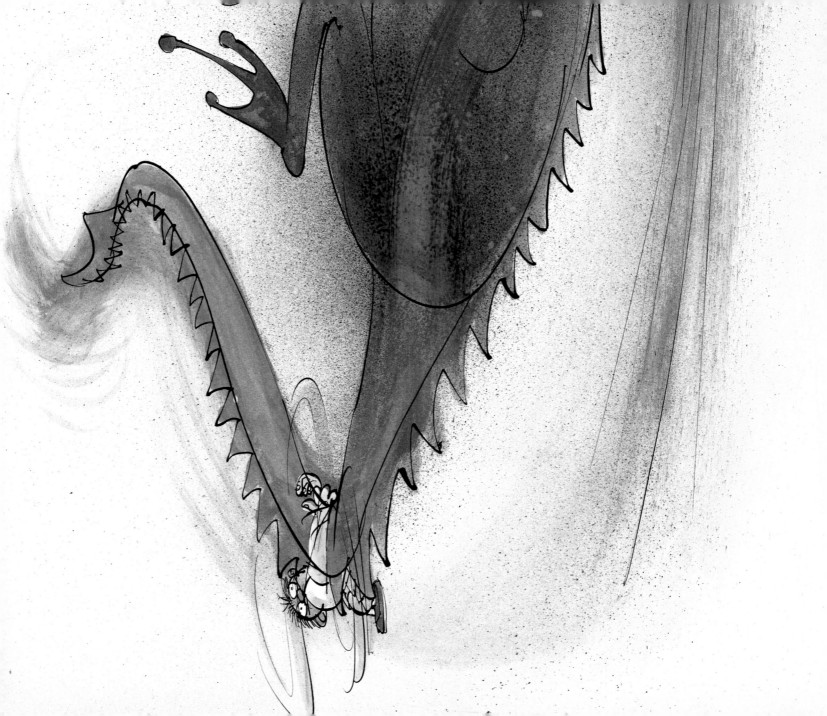

"A DINOSAUR?" said his mother.
"N-O-P-E!" said Tom.

"Well, HOW big, then?" asked his mother.
"Big enough to swing myself," replied Tom.

"Oh love, is that all?" said his mother. "Well, you get your coat on. I'll get the umbrella. We'll go for a swing in the rain."